Runner
for the
King

By ROWENA BENNETT

Illustrated by BOB MAGNUSEN

SCHOLASTIC  BOOK SERVICES

Published by Scholastic Book Services, a division
of Scholastic Magazines, Inc., New York, N. Y.

Copyright 1944 by Follett Publishing Company. Copyright © 1962 by Scholastic
Magazines, Inc. This edition is published by Scholastic Book Services, a division
of Scholastic Magazines, Inc., by arrangement with Follett Publishing Company.

3rd printing...January 1969

Printed in the U.S.A.

To Dory

Like a runner, running fast,
You and I, who share the past,
Glimpse in fragments as we run
Distant hills aflame with sun.

ROCA was running toward the sunset, rounding a curve in the mountains, racing down the longest road in the Andes. He was running as only an Indian boy can run, with light, springy steps. The fleet vicuña wondered at his swiftness. Even the condor, circling overhead, was surprised at his speed. For Roca was a *runner for the King*. This meant he had been found faster of foot than any boy in his province. So he had been given the honored task of bearing messages for the

Inca Emperor, the King of Kings, Son of the Sun.

Sometimes it was fresh fish from the sea that Roca carried for the Emperor's table — fish that swam in salt water in a waterproof basket till they reached the palace kitchen.

Sometimes it was a bundle of knotted string, called a *quipu*, that told the Emperor how many llama herds grazed on his hillsides, or how much the country folk owed him in taxes.

But the quipu Roca was bearing today carried the most important message of all. That was why he was running so fast. He could not read the knotted-string language. Only the *Villac Umu* (High Priest) and the Inca princes themselves could read this strange "writing." For they had been to school, and Roca had not. But the Indian boy knew from the color of the string that the message was urgent. Besides, an explanation had been whispered in his ear by the

last postboy when he handed Roca the bundle: "Jungle tribes are rising to make war on us. Spies have been seen in the northern and eastern provinces. The enemy plans to attack after dark tonight. Give warning to the Son of the Sun."

Roca clutched the bundle of string tighter. So many knots must mean a large army attacking. He shuddered. How terrible it would be to have the beautiful city of Cuzco overrun by savages and the good, kind Emperor taken prisoner!

Roca had seen the Emperor once, riding up the long stone road where he himself was now running. The Son of the Sun had been seated in a chair mounted on poles, a throne carried by sturdy Indians of great strength. There was a canopy of feathers over his head, and this canopy was carried by four nobles in elegant clothes, attendants of the King. It was a great honor to carry the litter or the canopy. Only brave men were chosen for this. There had been a procession, too, of warriors and priests and princes.

The Great Inca was dressed in feathers to match the canopy, feathers from the wings of every bright-colored bird in Inca Land. It was a wonderful sight. Roca had never forgotten it. But the thing he remembered best was the Emperor's smile. Such a warm, glowing smile! Like the smile of the sun as it looked down on the terraced farm lands of the Andes! No one could smile that way except the Son of the Sun.

And just as the sun in the heavens made the earth bear blossom and leaf and fruit, so the Great Inca and his fathers before him had made Inca Land bring forth cities and roads and bridges. So that now it was the greatest of all lands, and the best as well, thought Roca. For here no one knew poverty, or want, or hunger. Each man had his own work, yet none bore too heavy a burden. It was good to live in such a country, good to be in the service of so gracious a king.

Roca thought of the warning message and shuddered. He could picture fierce

jungle tribes swarming over the colorful countryside, frightening alpaca herds and destroying the ripening crops.

Such a thing must never happen. He himself must see that it did not happen. He must rush the message forward so fast that it would get to the palace before the savages could attack.

He quickened his step. He had supposed he was running at top speed. But his fearful thoughts whipped him to a faster pace. Farm lands that had been climbing the hills in giant stairs on each side of him now flowed past like colored waterfalls. Grazing llama herds had barely time to lift their heads and look at him before he was out of sight. Where the steepness of the grade turned the stone highway into stone stairs Roca bounded up the steps two at a time, or even scaled the whole flight with one running leap.

His red-brown body shone with perspiration, and his muscles rippled rhythmically. It was well he was not hindered or heated by clothing. He wore only a loincloth, and a headband to hold back his bobbed hair. His bare feet could grip the pavement better than if he wore sandals.

"If only I could take the message to the Emperor myself!" thought Roca. But his three-mile stint ended around the next curve in the mountains. There he would hand the quipu to the last post-runner, as one hands on the stick in a relay race. How lucky the last boy was! For he was a city boy and ran to and from Cuzco every day. He passed the Temple of the Sun, with its many stone steps, and the giant sundial that told time by moving a shadow finger, and entered the palace itself, where the King of Kings was seated upon the throne.

Roca had often wished that *his* was the last three-mile stint instead of the next to the last. But, while he was the fastest runner in the province, he was also the youngest. The Highland official who chose the runners was afraid Roca was too young to appear at the palace. He had said, "You would not know how to act in the presence of the Great Inça. You will have to wait until you are older before I can put you on the run to Cuzco." Roca made a face as he thought of it. He was sure he could learn what to do even in a great palace. He had been to Cuzco many times, taking his father's potatoes to market on the backs of llamas. He had not felt strange at all among the city people, only happy and excited.

Oh, well, he would not like to take the last stint away from Cachi, for Cachi was his good friend and had helped him to learn the ways of post-running. It was Cachi who had first told him about the barefoot express that tied all Inca Land together. Cachi's father had been a runner once. He was a city man, not a farmer like Roca's father. So Cachi had learned from his father the things he had taught to Roca. It made Roca wish very much that someday he could do something nice for Cachi.

In just a few minutes he would see his friend. Just one more bend in the mountain, and the posthouse would come into view.

He might be running toward the sunset now, but soon the road would straighten to the south and stretch out in the valley before him, thin as a parrot's feather and red with the last light of day.

Cachi would see him coming down the hillside and run to meet him. Then Roca would tell him the whispered warning and give him the bundle of knotted string. They would not visit as they ran this time, for Cachi would have to save his breath for speeding ahead, since the message was such an important one. Roca would be left behind. He would stumble into the post-house, panting hard, and fling himself on the stone floor, tired out, but wishing just the same that *he* were the one going to Cuzco to give the Emperor warning.

All this Roca was thinking as he rounded the curve in the mountains. Then, suddenly, he stopped short. For the road had stopped, too. The wonderful stone highway that

stretched from north to south the whole length of Inca Land now ended in a stone wall. For a minute Roca could not think what had happened. Then he realized there had been a landslide. A great rock from the slope above had become loosened and had rolled across the road below. It was a rock that would take many men to roll away, and on one side of it the mountain rose too steep to climb. On the other side lay a deep, dangerous ravine.

ROCA hesitated only a moment. Then he plunged into the dark shadows of the ravine. He knew that in those shadows wild beasts and serpents lurked. But the fear of them was as nothing compared to the fear of losing time. He would have to run at least half a mile down the ravine before there would be a slope gradual enough to allow him to climb back onto the road. As it was, the downward path where he now struggled caught him at every step with tangles of brush and

weed. It was all he could do to keep his footing. At the very bottom he stumbled and fell, tripping over something soft — soft and warm and furry against his bare feet.

When it cried out with a sharp kitten cry, he knew it was a baby puma. Somewhere across the gorge a catlike snarl answered. In a moment the mother would attack him with all the fury of a mountain lion protecting her cub. He must get to his feet before she sprang. That was the first thought that flashed through his mind.

Then the mother puma was upon him.

She came hurtling down from some rocky ledge, her yellow-green eyes flashing like meteors streaking across a night sky. Her hot breath fanned his cheek, her sharp claws gripped his shoulder. The weight of her body forced him to earth again. They rolled on the ground together, boy and beast.

All the strength of hunting and leaping was in the limbs of the puma — all the strength of running and farming, in the body of the boy. The match appeared to be equal. But there was one thing in the boy's favor — that which is in every human being's favor: his wit. It was because of human intelligence that Roca had a knife at his belt. It was because of his knowledge and experience that he knew exactly where the heart of the puma was located. Hadn't he skinned more than one lion and hung the hides on the walls of his hut? He knew how the creature was made inside. If only he could get his hand to his belt . . . There! The knife handle was in his grasp now. One quick plunge of the point, neither an inch to the left nor an inch to the right, but straight into the beating heart. Instantly the limbs of the great cat relaxed, its breath went out in a roaring sigh.

Roca lay for a long moment exhausted. Then he struggled out from under the weight of the animal's body. The thoughts that seemed to have whirled away from him suddenly were now whirling back: The message! The knotted string! The danger to Cuzco and the Emperor! How disgraceful it would be to fail in his duty as post-runner. He must run, run, run to make up for this delay. He did not think of the blood oozing and dripping from his shoulder, or the marks of the puma's fangs spotting his arms, or the throbbing bruises on his legs. He began to search nervously for the quipu, groping about the ground with his hands. The depth of the darkness frightened him. Night was coming fast — night and the approaching attack of savages.

At last his hand clutched the bundle, and in no time he was moving down the gorge recklessly — crashing, wading, stumbling — heeding neither rock nor hole nor living peril.

The late light of the day above began to glimmer more clearly through thinning trees. The sides of the gorge widened and became more gentle. Roca was about to scramble up to the highway again when he heard voices above him — strange voices that made him pause and draw back into the shadow. Some inner warning told Roca that it might be safer to wait before showing himself.

Three men were coming up the road. They were clad as Inca officials. But something about them was wrong. It was not their dress. They all wore the gold earrings and fine sandals common to men of their rank. One was clad in the long woven robe of the seashore, a cotton robe striped in tan and brown. He had a crownlike hat upon his head and carried a gold-headed staff such as a seaside nobleman would be apt to carry.

Another was dressed all in feathers woven together like a fabric of bright design. This was correct for an eastern slope dweller.

The third wore the clothes of Roca's own Highland official: a short vicuña-wool tunic and a feather headdress. His walk, however, was unfamiliar, and this was not as it should have been. For Roca himself knew the Highland official, had been hired by him just recently, had taken orders from him and carried messages, had seen him wearing these very clothes. This man did not look like him, though his face was turned away and the Indian boy could not be sure. Perhaps the Highlander was sick, and someone else was taking his place.

Roca listened attentively as the three men came nearer. Then he knew what was wrong. It was their language. They were not speaking Quechuan, which was the official language of Inca Land. Instead they were talking in some strange tongue whose accents fell harshly on Roca's sensitive ears. He waited till they had turned the corner before he climbed out onto the road. He felt uneasy about the matter and was glad to be on his way without being seen.

Out of the ravine, Roca found it was lighter than he had expected. The sun had not quite dropped. But a faintness seemed to be coming over the Indian boy, and he realized for the first time that he was losing blood. No matter! He was in sight of the posthouse now. Cachi would be coming to meet him. His own work would soon be done.

Yet, as he reached the valley, no runner came forward up the stone highway. No sign of life showed itself about the thatch-roofed stone building. A strange fear of new trouble swept over Roca. He sped forward fearfully, dizzily.

When he crossed the threshold of the posthouse, he found it empty.

ROCA's first impulse was to call Cachi's name. But some inner warning stopped him. Making a quiet search would be wiser. He hurried outside. He had not far to go. Back of the house he found Cachi, lying on the ground bound and gagged.

"Cachi! Cachi! How did this happen?" Roca was cutting his friend's bonds with the knife that had killed the puma. He was unwinding the cloth that kept Cachi from answering.

"It was spies, Roca, spies! They are everywhere! Strange Indians in disguise!" Cachi was sitting up now, rubbing the sore stripes made by the pressing rope. "Someone is plotting against our Emperor, against our own Inca Land—"

"Yes, yes, I know. The jungle tribes will attack tonight. This is the message I bear. Did these spies go on to Cuzco?"

"No, back up the road to meet you. They would have bound you, too. How did they miss you?"

"A rock fell across my path," explained Roca, "a large rock they will not be able to push away unless they are many."

"They are only three, dressed as Inca officials —"

"What? So that is it! Those officials are spies. I knew there was something wrong when they didn't speak our language."

"You saw them?"

"Yes. But they did not see me."

"How did that happen? How did you pass the fallen rock?"

"Through the ravine and up the slope half a mile down. I was in the ravine when the three men walked by."

"Good! They will think you could not get around the landslide. Perhaps they will give up pursuing you."

"Then they will come back this way. No doubt they are going to Cuzco. You must be quick, Cachi. Take the knotted string. Be on the road at once."

Cachi shook his head. "I cannot go. I wrenched my ankle as I tried to run away from them. I think I have a bad sprain." He said it as though it were a nuisance, a handicap, not a pain. A brave boy, Cachi. Roca looked at him proudly. It was good to have such a friend. He stretched out a hand.

"Here," he said, "let me help you as far as the woodland. Then you can crawl home to Cuzco through the bushes."

"No," said Cachi, "that would delay you. There is not a moment to lose. I shall hop home from here. If I am fast enough on two feet to be a post-runner, I shall be fast enough on one to keep ahead of trouble. But what about you, Roca? Are you able to go another three miles? You look very tired and are still panting. What is that stain upon your shoulder? I cannot see in this half-light, but it looks like blood."

"I had a little struggle with a puma in the ravine. It was nothing. The blood is clotted now. And a lame shoulder will not keep one from running as a lame foot must."

With that, Roca tucked the *quipu* into his belt and was on the road again, hurrying, hurrying, hurrying toward Cuzco. The ache had left his limbs, the pain was gone from his shoulder. He felt light as a feather blowing down the wind. After all, it was he himself who would carry the message to the King!

But would he get there in time? The savages were to strike after dark. How soon after dark, he wondered. The red daylight that still lingered on the tops of the hills was gone from the valleys. Dusk, thick as llama's hair, gathered about him. His wet body shivered. His hair became stringy with dew. He found himself praying desperately to the Sun God: "Give me, O Sun, thy pure and sacred fire! Let it not burn out, but flame in the heavens till this, thy servant, has reached Cuzco. It is thy son, O Sun, who faces danger. Hold up thy light."

As he finished the prayer, it seemed to Roca that the afterglow of the sunset dyed the distant mountain peaks a deeper red and that the far lakes flashed sudden gold. Had the Sun God heard his cry?

In the midst of his wondering, someone called his name: "Roca, Roca!" It was a low, muffled call — so muffled that if it had been any name but his own the Indian boy would not have been halted by the sound. He would have dismissed it as the smothered cry of a young alpaca drawing closer to its mother in the darkness. But one hears his own name even in a half whisper and responds to it without second thought. That was what Roca did. He stopped short and looked about.

"Who calls me?" he cried.

Then the voice came again, weakly moaning, "Here, Roca, here. Help me."

It came from the roadside, where the shadows were thickest. Through the blackness Roca walked toward the sound. He felt around on the earth with his hands. A man's half-clad body met his touch, then another, and another. Three men lay bound and gagged as Cachi had lain. Now that his eyes were accustomed to the dark, Roca saw them quite clearly. One was his own Highland official.

Roca whipped out his knife again and set about freeing his superior officer. He freed the proud fellow's hands first, and immediately the man tore off his loosened mouth gag and quickly removed his friend's gags. What angry mouths were released! These men did not take their captivity as bravely as Cachi had. They seemed monstrously insulted. For they were used to having people do their bidding, rather than being forced to do the bidding of others. But after they had sputtered a string of useless words against their assailants (who, of course, were nowhere in sight), the Highland official turned to Roca and said less harshly, "Whatever should I have done if you had not come along? I heard your quick running step as you flew down the road. I knew no one could run like that save Roca."

The Indian boy smiled to himself. This great man had never praised him before. Instead he had treated him like a child.

"It was Cachi I was listening for," continued the official. "He was due here any moment — overdue in fact. Where is he? How does it happen you are running in his place?"

THEN Roca explained what had happened to Cachi, and was not surprised to learn that the same three men who had bound him had also bound the Highland official.

"Not only did they attack me and rob me of my clothes," complained the official, crossly, "but as you see, they did the same to my two friends, an official from the coast and one from the eastern slopes."

"Yes, I saw the villains wearing official clothes," said Roca. And he told of his experience in the ravine.

"We should have been a match for them if they had not taken us by surprise," declared the Highlander. "But they jumped on us from the bushes when we were strolling along, suspecting nothing. It is the first time in many a day I have met robbers in Inca Land."

"But they are *worse* than robbers," cried Roca. "They are spies!" He told of the message he was carrying: "That is why I must leave you here and hurry on," he explained. "There, the last of your cords is cut!"

The official looked dazed. "But my two friends!" he cried. "You must help me unbind them."

"I'm sorry," said Roca firmly, "but I cannot stop to help your friends. You will have to help them yourself. Here is my knife to cut their bonds." And tossing the weapon into the official's lap, he was off again on the road.

How had he dared to talk to a nobleman like that, he wondered. He had told him what to do, instead of taking his orders. Perhaps he would lose his job as post-runner now. He bit his lip at the thought. But what was that to losing Cuzco and his King? Yes. He had done the right thing, even if he had seemed rude. This thought gave him new courage.

It was getting very late. But surely there would be no more delays now, and the city was not far distant. Only a bend and a dip in the road, then the hanging bridge, and he was there.

If only his legs did not feel so numb and his shoulder throb so! Again he prayed to

the Sun God, but this time the god seemed far away, gone over the edge of night. His sister-wife, the moon goddess, was showing her pale white face. He would have prayed to her instead, but what good could she do him? Her light was not strength-giving like the light of the sun. She could not pull the flowers out of the seed nor the great trees up

from the earth as the sun did. She could only smile and shine and hold her jeweled head high like a *coya,* or empress.

Roca saw the bridge now. It hung in a dark loop across a deep ravine, as a serpent hangs from a jungle tree. How thin it looked! How wide was the chasm below it! "Whenever I cross it," thought Roca, "I feel like a

spider running across the air on a single thread."

Did it swing and sway more than usual as he set foot upon it, he wondered, or was he so dizzy with hurrying that it only seemed to do so? He tried looking up at the stars rather than down at the blackness below. There was something terrifying about black, empty space. It made him feel smaller and smaller as he ran. When he was in the middle of the bridge, he suddenly seemed like a fly crossing a canyon.

At that very moment there was a loud, snapping sound and a quick, fearful jerking.

Roca rocked this way and that. He reached for the railing at his side and grasped it with both hands. The runway was slipping from under him. He felt his feet swinging out into nothingness. At first he could not think what had happened. Then, all at once, he knew that one of the aloe cables had broken, and only the other remained intact. The bridge was hanging by a single cable. Roca himself was hanging to that cable.

He remembered with a chill how far down the bottom of the gorge was and how sharp the rocks were there.

He remembered the message to the Emperor, and wondered if the bundle of knotted string was still tucked in his belt. Yes. He could feel the knots thumping against him. But how could he possibly get the quipu to the palace now?

Then he thought of the savages taking Cuzco by surprise, just as the three spies had captured the three officials. Surprise was the thing that made little armies win against big armies. No one in Cuzco would be expecting an attack. They would go to bed unsuspecting. Then suddenly the thatched roofs of the city would be burning and wild men would be yelling in the streets. It would be too late to get the King's warriors together, and the guards would have been tied up by spies. Hadn't Cachi said spies were everywhere?

The Temple of the Sun would be raided and the sacred golden goblets stolen. The market place would be plundered and haunches of llama meat and sacks of potatoes strewn about everywhere. Roca could see it in his mind. But worst of all, he could see the Emperor himself being carried off by his enemies, carried in disgrace toward the eastern jungle land.

No, no! This must never be! As the picture flashed before him, he began to move hand over hand along the rope, swinging his body back and forth to gain momentum. He might be dangling in mid-air, but he was going forward toward the bank, toward the other end of the bridge.

He now became vaguely aware of lights on the opposite bluff. A group of men with flaming torches stood along the bank. For a moment Roca's heart failed him. He paused doubtfully. Could these be the savages come to destroy? No, surely not. For if they were, they would be setting fire to the bridge, and they made no move to do so. They must be friends instead. This thought gave him courage, and he renewed his effort to go forward.

But a sudden pain shot through his shoulder. The blood began to gush forth again from the wound inflicted by the puma. A giddiness swept over the sturdy body of the Indian boy. His fingers felt cramped and numb. They could not seem to clench the rope. Soon they would lose their hold. The flickering torches shone brighter on the bank

ahead. There was only a little way to go. But
Roca could no longer draw himself forward.
His strength was gone.

THEN a voice came to him across the darkness—a friendly, Quechuan-speaking voice. "Hang on," it said. "You're almost here."

It was so cheerful, so reassuring, it seemed to warm him through and through even to his numb finger tips. A strength flowed over him that was not the strength of the body, but that of the mind, kindled by hope. His hands moved on once more. Suddenly the bank seemed to come down to meet him. A loud cheering greeted his ears. Admiring eyes looked into his. *He was there!*

He climbed up onto the solid ground. He could hear himself saying desperately: "The Emperor! Important news! Life and death..."

Then he was raised to the shoulders of the crowd and borne through the streets of Cuzco toward the palace.

But the palace hall that he had wanted so much to see was only a blur to him, and the Great Inca a dim figure. Even his own voice sounded faint and far away as he threw himself down before the throne and cried out his message.

With fumbling fingers he felt for the bundle of knotted string and laid it at the Emperor's feet. Then the room whirled round him, and he fell forward on his face, fainting.

When Roca came to, he found himself in a beautiful chamber, the stone walls of which were ornamented with gold — gold that hurt his eyes because it was flashing the light of day.

Yes, night was gone, and day streamed through the deep-set, odd-shaped windows of the palace. For of course so grand a room could only be in a palace or a temple.

Over Roca was bending an important-looking man, the doctor-herbalist. He was putting good-smelling herbs on the Indian boy's shoulder and binding it up with a soft cotton cloth.

Roca was trying to remember all that had taken place the night before. He drew his eyebrows together in a puzzled frown. Then he said quickly, "The savages! They must have been turned back. It is so quiet here. Or is there a battle going on outside the city?"

"Hush!" said the doctor-herbalist. "All is well. You must rest." The doctor tiptoed quietly out of the room.

Roca was angry. He forgot to be impressed by the great man.

"I will run after him," he thought, and he tried to jump up out of his soft blanket bed. However, he fell back again with a cry. Not only was his shoulder stabbing him, but the aches of his stiff muscles and many bruises turned his whole body into one pulsing pain. He would wait awhile before getting up. In a short time he would be himself again.

He listened to the doctor's footsteps dying away in the distance. Then he heard other feet coming toward him. Two firm ones, two limping ones.

A servant appeared and bowed low. Behind him came Cachi.

Could it be the servant was bowing Cachi into the room, just as though he were a great nobleman?

Roca did not know. He did not stop to figure it out. He did not care. He was too happy to see his friend to bother about how he got there.

"Cáchi, Cachi! I'm so glad you came. You are going to take me to *your* house in Cuzco, I know. But tell me first all that has happened! What of the savages? What of the spies? Is the battle still on?"

Cachi came over and sat down by him. He put his lame ankle on a soft corner of Roca's blanket. The ankle was tightly bound. He said quietly, "You mustn't get excited, Roca. The doctor-herbalist says I cannot stay with you if I excite you."

Roca tried to look calm. "Tell me everything in a soft voice," he said.

Cachi coughed and cleared his throat. "The savages were driven back just in time," he whispered. "They were at the edge of the city when our warriors met them."

"And what of the spies?"

"They were captured by the three officials whom they had robbed—the ones you set free."

"I only had time to help one of them—our own Highland nobleman. I was afraid he might not like the hurried way I left him—"

Cachi laughed. "If he didn't, he has gotten over it now. He is boasting to everybody that *he* was the one who chose you for a post-runner."

Roca laughed, too. "Perhaps he will not always be telling me how young I am, now." He lay back against his blankets with a happy sigh. He had won the race with time after all.

"How kind of the Emperor to let me stay here last night!" he said. "How good of him to send the doctor to me!"

"He is a good, kind Emperor," beamed Cachi.

"But now I feel strong enough to go with you to your house," said Roca, for he thought Cachi had come to fetch him. He flexed the muscles of his arms. "See, I am not so stiff. I shall even be strong enough to run again at the end of this day."

Cachi smiled, and as he did so Roca saw there was a secret in his face, hiding behind his eyes. A good secret. He wondered what it was. Perhaps Cachi would tell it to him on the way home.

It was then that two servants came into the room with a golden litter. They bowed low to Roca. "The Son of the Sun wishes to see you," they said. "He has sent his golden litter for you."

Roca's dark eyes grew big with surprise. "The Emperor wishes to see *me?*"

The two servants nodded. "That is the King's order."

"I shall help you from the bed," said Cachi, offering a hand.

"But," protested Roca, addressing himself to the servants, "I gave the Emperor my message last night. I have no new one."

Cachi answered. "That doesn't matter. The King wishes to thank you in person for what you have done."

Roca gasped. He looked deep into Cachi's eyes to be sure he was not joking. Then he saw that *this* was the secret his friend had been hiding there.

His heart did a relay race all its own. If he had expected any thanks at all it was in the form of a word or two from the Highland official, not from the Great Inca himself.

He said firmly, "I shall walk to the throne room. A post-runner shall not ride on a litter. Litters are for princes only."

This time Roca saw the Emperor quite clearly. He was not dressed all in feathers as he had once seen him, though a crown of feathers did rise from his golden helmet. He wore a finely woven, shining robe with a collar as scalloped as the sun's rays, and from his neck on a golden chain hung a golden puma. In his hand was a long staff at the end of which the image of the sun blazed.

With this staff he touched the kneeling Roca gently.

"Runner for the King," he said, "you have served me well. Even to the saving of my empire..."

Roca gasped. He had not thought of himself as the savior of an empire. "Oh no!" he cried. "I only did my duty."

The Inca smiled. "If all citizens did their duty," he said, "there would be no lost kingdom in all the world."

He paused, then asked kindly, "What reward would you like for this service, Roca?"

The Indian boy looked surprised. "I need no reward," he said. "It is enough to be a post-runner. I like it better than anything I know. It is good to have the feel of the stone road under my feet. To run up the brown hills and down the green valleys. To see the farm lands go by and the llama herds grazing. It is fun to leap across the wide ravine on a swinging—"

"Bridge?" The Emperor was laughing now, and his laugh made Roca think of sunlight on water. "I heard how you crossed the bridge last night. It is well I sent my men out to watch for a late runner. For they saw a wonderful sight, a feat of strength and valor. I wish I might have beheld so brave a crossing, myself."

The Inca's eyes grew suddenly serious. "Did you know, Roca, that the bridge had been cut by our enemies? They partially severed one aloe cable so that my army would get halfway over before sensing the danger. They did not know how much they had weakened the whole. They did not know the rhythm of one boy's pounding feet would loosen the structure. They did not know one boy could save a whole army. This is another reason I wish to reward you, Roca."

With that the Son of the Sun took the golden puma from the chain around his neck and placed it in Roca's hand.

"I understand," he said, "that you are as good at wrestling pumas as crossing bridges."

"You seem to know everything!" exclaimed Roca in amazement that the Emperor even knew of his meeting the puma.

"I have talked with Cachi and the Highland official and others," said the Inca. "I know, too, that you would like as your stint the last run of the day to Cuzco."

"But that is Cachi's run!" cried Roca.

Again the Emperor smiled. "Perhaps Cachi would rather serve me in another way," he said. "He has chosen to be one of my litter carriers."

Roca found Cachi's face across the room among many strange faces. He saw that it was a very happy face. He knew Cachi had chosen what he wanted most.

"You are sure you do not wish to change your own mind?" asked the Inca.

"No," said Roca. "I like running best."

"Good!" cried the Emperor. "Now I shall feel safer on my throne than I have ever felt in all my life before."